The Lilac Lesson

PRAISE FOR *STORYSHARES*

"One of the brightest innovators and game-changers in the education industry."
– Forbes

"Your success in applying research-validated practices to promote literacy serves as a valuable model for other organizations seeking to create evidence-based literacy programs."

- Library of Congress

"We need powerful social and educational innovation, and Storyshares is breaking new ground. The organization addresses critical problems facing our students and teachers. I am excited about the strategies it brings to the collective work of making sure every student has an equal chance in life."
– Teach For America

"Around the world, this is one of the up-and-coming trailblazers changing the landscape of literacy and education."
- International Literacy Association

"It's the perfect idea. There's really nothing like this. I mean wow, this will be a wonderful experience for young people."   - Andrea Davis Pinkney, Executive Director, Scholastic

"Reading for meaning opens opportunities for a lifetime of learning. Providing emerging readers with engaging texts that are designed to offer both challenges and support for each individual will improve their lives for years to come. Storyshares is a wonderful start."
- David Rose, Co-founder of CAST & UDL

The Lilac Lesson

Cat Jenkins

STORYSHARES

Story Share, Inc.
New York. Boston. Philadelphia

Storyshares
Story Share, Inc.
24 N. Bryn Mawr Avenue #340
Bryn Mawr, PA 19010-3304
www.storyshares.org

Inspiring reading with a new kind of book.

Interest Level: High School
Grade Level Equivalent: 4.6

9781642615357

Book design by Storyshares

Printed in the United States of America

Storyshares Presents

1

That spring, the lilacs hung heavy and fragrant. That was the spring that they finally had a name for what was wrong with Sandy.

It was a relief, like all the people around her had been holding their breath all her life. Now they could finally let it out. They had a label for her. At last, at last, at last.

Autism. Asperger's.

The only one who wasn't relieved was Sandy. All grown up, all on her own Sandy. Shy Sandy, who hated going to parties. Silent Sandy, who never spoke up or raised her hand in class. Weird Sandy, who never caught the undercurrents of conversations or jokes. Odd Sandy, who got through school with high marks and no friends. Strange Sandy, who watched everyone and copied what they did but still didn't blend in.

Sandy sat on the balcony of her tiny apartment, watching the lilacs sway in the breeze. She thought about what it meant to be safely stowed away in a box with a label.

I'm smart. I'm creative. I just . . . like being alone.

It was so much easier than trying to get through the social maze that others seemed to navigate effortlessly. Even when she copied how others smiled and nodded, Sandy felt as though she was speaking a foreign language. She knew others could tell it wasn't natural for her. She was . . . different.

2

Sandy closed her eyes and thought of last Christmas. It was like touching a bruise; something about the pain was secretly satisfying.

It had been a family Christmas. Mom, Dad, Sandy, her older brother Rob, and Rob's wife, Cathy. Everything had been normal until late on Christmas Eve when Sandy overheard the whispered conversation between Rob and their mother.

"So is Sandy *ever* gonna get married?" Rob's low voice was full of smug superiority.

"I don't know. She's not like you, dear," Mom murmured.

But even Sandy could detect the note of longing in her mother's words. Of course she wanted her only daughter to settle down with a spouse and a family of her own.

Sandy wasn't against meeting someone special. She just didn't know how.

If I can't even make friends, how am I supposed to have a romantic relationship? How can someone fall in love with me? Sandy thought.

Sandy slunk away before she could hear anything else. She already felt like she wasn't living up to her family's expectations. She didn't need to hear any more.

The next morning, on Christmas Day, they exchanged gifts.

"Here," Cathy said with a grin as she handed a package to her sister-in-law. "Merry Christmas, Sandy!"

Curious, Sandy picked apart the seams of Scotch tape and peeled back the festive wrapping paper. It was a large, old-fashioned wicker picnic basket. It was bright white and was decorated with vines and silky pink roses.

"Open it," Cathy said, her eyes glowing with anticipation.

Inside were paper plates, cutlery, napkins, and a pair of elegant wine glasses. Sandy ran her fingers over the curious contents. *What am I supposed to do with this?* she thought, but she returned Cathy's smile.

"It's beautiful. Thank you." Sandy knew that was the correct response, no matter whether or not the gift made sense.

"Now all you have to do is find someone to take on a nice romantic picnic," Cathy announced, looking as though she'd found the solution to a difficult problem.

Sandy wasn't good at hiding her real emotions. She could copy other people's reactions, but it was almost impossible to make these imitations seem natural.

Sensing the blankness behind Sandy's smile, Cathy explained, "It's so you'll go out and find someone to marry. You *do* want to get married someday, don't you?"

Sandy nodded and kept her eyes fixed on the pretty, rose-covered basket.

It felt like a dagger in Sandy's heart. *Just go out and find someone? This basket is supposed to make it easier to do that?* The dagger twisted a little. *That's like asking me if I want to travel and then putting me in the cockpit of a jet and telling me 'this is all you need to get there. Just do it.'*

It had hurt that no one, not even her family, understood her. *If it was that simple, I'd have friends. I'd be going out all the time and would meet people. I'd walk out on the street every morning and feel like I'm part of it all.*

3

It was after that awful, painful Christmas that Sandy had finally gone to her doctor. She let her confusion and hurt spill all over the place like a burst water pipe. It had been hard. She'd felt ashamed and worse than ever.

But the doctor knew what questions to ask and what patterns to recognize. And now Sandy had a label. Asperger's. Something that fell on the autism scale. Wasn't it a shame that they didn't recognize things like that while Sandy was growing up? Her life might have been quite different.

Sandy was unsure about how to move forward now that she had this label, this medically defined box in which to live her never-quite-normal life.

Sandy sat on the balcony of her apartment and watched the lilacs nod and bend in the breeze. She breathed in their heady scent. Then Sandy remembered...

Granny Tess.

4

Granny Tess wasn't really Sandy's grandmother. She was a neighbor who had lived a few houses down from Sandy's parents when Sandy was growing up. Granny Tess and Sandy had bonded right from the start.

Tess had noticed the quiet little girl who didn't seem to mind playing alone. Granny Tess was different, too. She'd had a reputation for her flower garden, but it was more than that. Granny Tess spent all her time among her herbs and shrubs, her vines and trees. Nicer people said she was a "naturalist," who studied the ways and meanings of plants. Not-so-nice people called her a "kitchen witch," who brewed old-time folk medicines and knew the secrets that plants could tell.

Granny Tess liked her solitude, but she didn't mind visiting with the shy little girl who played alone.

With the wisdom that comes from watching nature, Granny Tess seemed to know the right words when Sandy needed to hear them. Sandy was drawn to the lush lilac bushes that stood like fragrant guards along the edges of Granny Tess's garden. Granny Tess let Sandy stare at the tiny blossoms for as long as her heart desired.

5

"Beautiful, aren't they?" Granny Tess took a break from weeding and stood beside Sandy.

Deep purple, pale lavender, delicate pink, creamy white, violet blue. Sandy felt overwhelmed by it all. Where was one to look when beauty was everywhere? Robbed of speech, as she so often was, Sandy merely nodded. *Yes, they are so very, very beautiful.*

Granny Tess lived among her plants. She knew the impact they could have on people who took the time to look. She also knew that when you felt too much and words got all tangled up, it helped to focus on one tiny thing. Just one. Like a key that could open a gate. Like a single sunbeam that could warm and calm you.

Granny Tess pulled down a branch of the darkest, most royal-looking purple lilacs. She bent them so they were right in front of Sandy's eyes.

"All plants have secrets," Granny Tess whispered, her voice as soft as a breeze. "If you're quiet enough and still enough, you can generally find them out."

Granny Tess bent closer. Her words were meant only for the ears of someone worthy. "Would you like to know the lilac's secret?"

Again, Sandy nodded.

"Alright. I'll tell you."

The tiny blossoms quivered as Granny Tess tried to hold them nearer still. "Look at them. Every flower has four petals. That's what lilacs are supposed to have. Four petals. But . . . look . . ."

With a gentle fingertip, Granny Tess prodded one little lilac out from where it was hiding among its four-petaled kin. "This one has five petals."

Under her breath, Sandy counted. *Yes. Five.* She gave Granny Tess a questioning glance.

"Sometimes you can find one with six petals, too." Granny Tess breathed a deep, content sigh. "The five- and six-petaled flowers stand out. They're not 'normal.' But they *are* beautiful. It's more fun to look at those ordinary four-petaled flowers when you know you might find something different and special among them. It's fun to think that you might be one of the lucky few to notice the differences."

Sandy-back-then spent a great many hours searching through Granny Tess's lilacs. She was always on the lookout for those rare little treasures.

Sandy-right-now looked at the lilacs growing over her balcony railing. She often tried to find a blossom that had extra petals. Her eyes traced over the graceful, nodding bunches . . . and froze.

6

Sandy leaned in closer, squinting her eyes to be sure she was seeing things right. From within a crowd of simple, four-petaled flowers, a tiny five-petaled lilac winked out at her. And beside it...another. Two of them, nestled together. A slow smile spread across her face.

Maybe a label wasn't such a bad thing. It might be what helped like-labeled people find each other.

Sandy's smile widened. She decided then and there that whatever they called her, she wouldn't think of herself as autistic or having Asperger's. She would think of herself as a lilac; a five-petaled beauty made special by the overwhelming presence of ordinary people.

There wouldn't have been a label waiting if it was just her. There were other five-petaled lilacs out there. She was not alone. And she was beautiful.

About The Author

Cat Jenkins lives in the Pacific Northwest where the weather is often conducive to long hours before a keyboard. Her stories in humor, fantasy, speculative fiction, and horror have been published both online and in print. Her first novel, *Sara When She Chooses*, was published by Bedazzled Ink Publishing in May 2018.

About The Publisher

Story Shares is a nonprofit focused on supporting the millions of teens and adults who struggle with reading by creating a new shelf in the library specifically for them. The ever-growing collection features content that is compelling and culturally relevant for teens and adults, yet still readable at a range of lower reading levels.

Story Shares generates content by engaging deeply with writers, bringing together a community to create this new kind of book. With more intriguing and approachable stories to choose from, the teens and adults who have fallen behind are improving their skills and beginning to discover the joy of reading. For more information, visit storyshares.org.

Easy to Read. Hard to Put Down.

www.ingramcontent.com/pod-product-compliance
Lightning Source LLC
Chambersburg PA
CBHW071231170626
46809CB00005BA/2036